P.K. HALLINAN
Let's Care About Sharing!

For Alan and Carol Garner,
who lovingly share their friendship,
their laughter, and their lives.
Blessings.

Ideals Children's Books
Nashville, Tennessee
an imprint of Hambleton-Hill Publishing, Inc.

Published by Ideals Children's Books
An imprint of Hambleton-Hill Publishing, Inc.
Nashville, Tennessee 37218

Printed and bound in the United States of America

Library of Congress Cataloging-in-Publication Data

Hallinan, P.K.
    Let's care about sharing! / by P.K. Hallinan, [author and
illustrator].
       p.   cm.
    Summary: P.K., Sue, and their friends discover the joy of sharing,
not only material things, but also their joys, sadnesses, dreams,
and themselves.
    ISBN 1-57102-105-1
    [1. Sharing—Fiction.] I. Title.
PZ7.H15466Le   1997
[E]—dc20   96-38781
                                              CIP
                                              AC

E

"I'm having fun too!"
Sue laughed, as she raced
his shiny red dump truck
all over the place.

"But here's what I think—
before the fun ends,
let's share about sharing
with *all* of our friends!"

So P.K. and Sue
knew just what to do.

First, they found Jeannie,
out washing her cat.

Then they found Henry,
retaping his bat.

And Ben was out working
especially hard,
pulling up dandelions
all over his yard.

"What's the big news?"
asked Ben, quite amused.

And P.K. chimed in,
"I bet if we dare,
we each could find something
real special to share!"

So the kids all replied,
"Let's give it a try!"

First came the toys,
as each one exchanged
a favorite plaything,
from tugboats to trains.

Then came the games,
like Parcheesi and chess,
with everyone vying
and trying their best.

They shared stamp collections.
They shared comic books.

They shared favorite costumes,
with hilarious looks.

They even shared savings—
pooled nickels and dimes—
to go to a movie called
Revenge of the Slime!

And the popcorn was hot,
hitting just the right spot.

"Sharing," said Jeannie,
outside on the street,
"really means more
than just movies and treats.

"I'm certain that there's
something deeper to share."

And so they shared feelings
and personal things.
They shared little heartaches
and the sadness they bring.

They shared private dreams
and felt so much better
when everyone nodded
and smiled together.

They shared in their work.

They shared in their play.
They cared about sharing
for the rest of the day.

And when they were through,
and evening was nigh,
they shared what they'd learned,
as they gazed at the sky.

"Sharing," said Henry,
"reminds me of stars.
  When they all shine together
  they're brighter by far!"